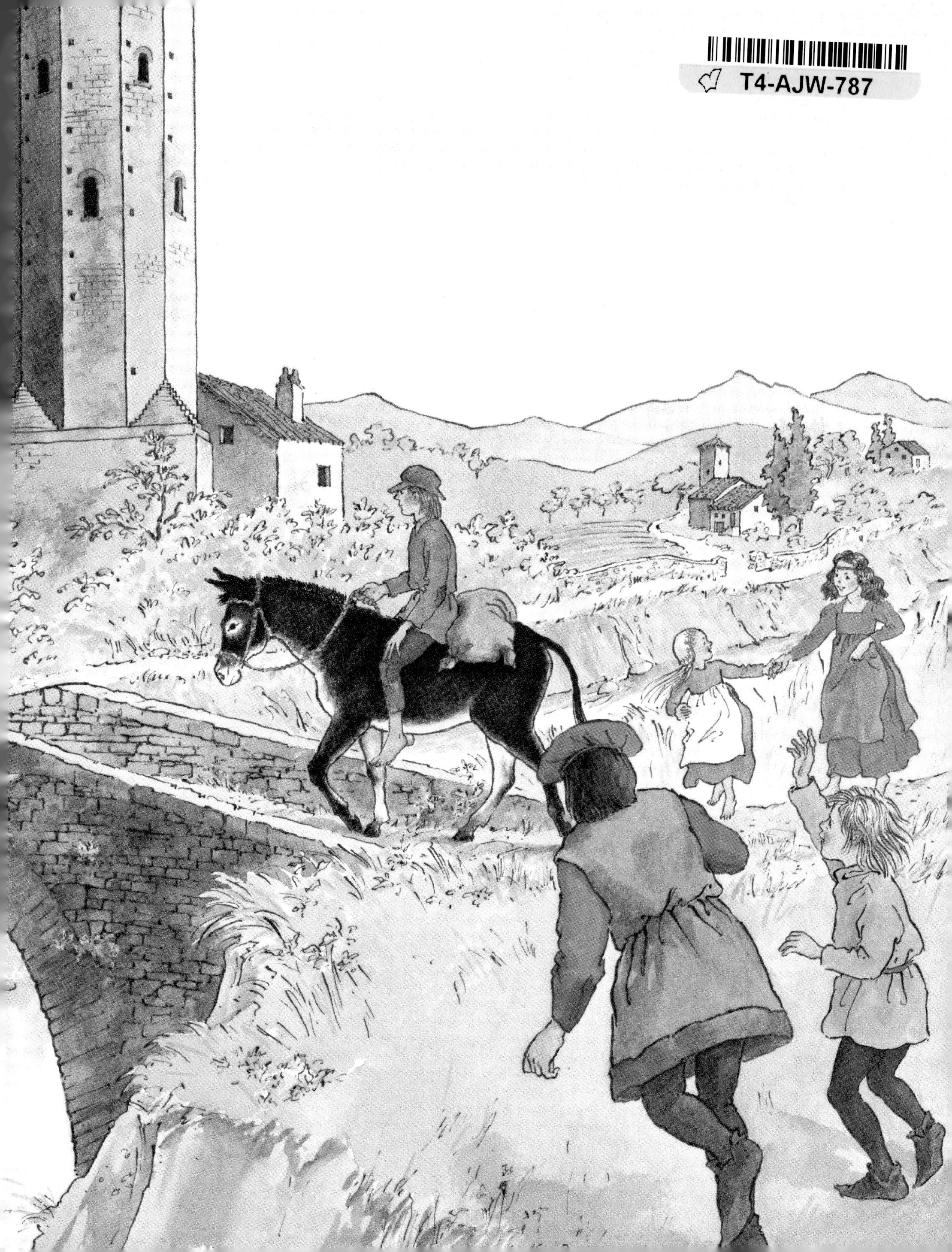

The Moon's Choice

The Moon's Choice

By John Warren Stewig
Illustrated by Jan Palmer

SIMON & SCHUSTER BOOKS FOR YOUNG READERS
Published by Simon & Schuster
New York   London   Toronto   Sydney   Tokyo   Singapore

This tale is based upon one found in *Novelle
Popolari Bolognesi*, published in Bologna, Italy in 1885,
compiled by Carolina Coronedi-Berti.
The Northern Italian language of that version shows
Austrian and French influences, as well. The
author acknowledges the help of Dr. Diana Bartley
with the translation.

SIMON & SCHUSTER BOOKS FOR YOUNG READERS
Simon & Schuster Building, Rockefeller Center
1230 Avenue of the Americas, New York, New York 10020.
Text copyright © 1993 by John Warren Stewig.
Illustrations copyright © 1993 by Jan Palmer.
SIMON & SCHUSTER BOOKS FOR YOUNG READERS
is a trademark of Simon & Schuster.
Designed by Vicki Kalajian.
The text for this book was set in Garamond Light.
The illustrations were done in watercolor.
Manufactured in the United States of America

10 9 8 7 6 5 4 3 2 1

Library of Congress Cataloging-in-Publication Data
Stewig, John W.   The moon's choice / by John Warren Stewig;
illustrated by Jan Palmer.   Summary: With the aid of the friendly moon,
Giricoccola survives the jealousy of her sisters
and the magic spells of a witch.
[1. Fairy tales.]   I. Palmer, Jan, ill.   II. Title.
PZ8.S64Mo   1993   [E]—dc20   CIP   91-43462
ISBN 0-671-76962-6

To Dagmar,
for early and continuing encouragement
— JWS

For Laura
— JP

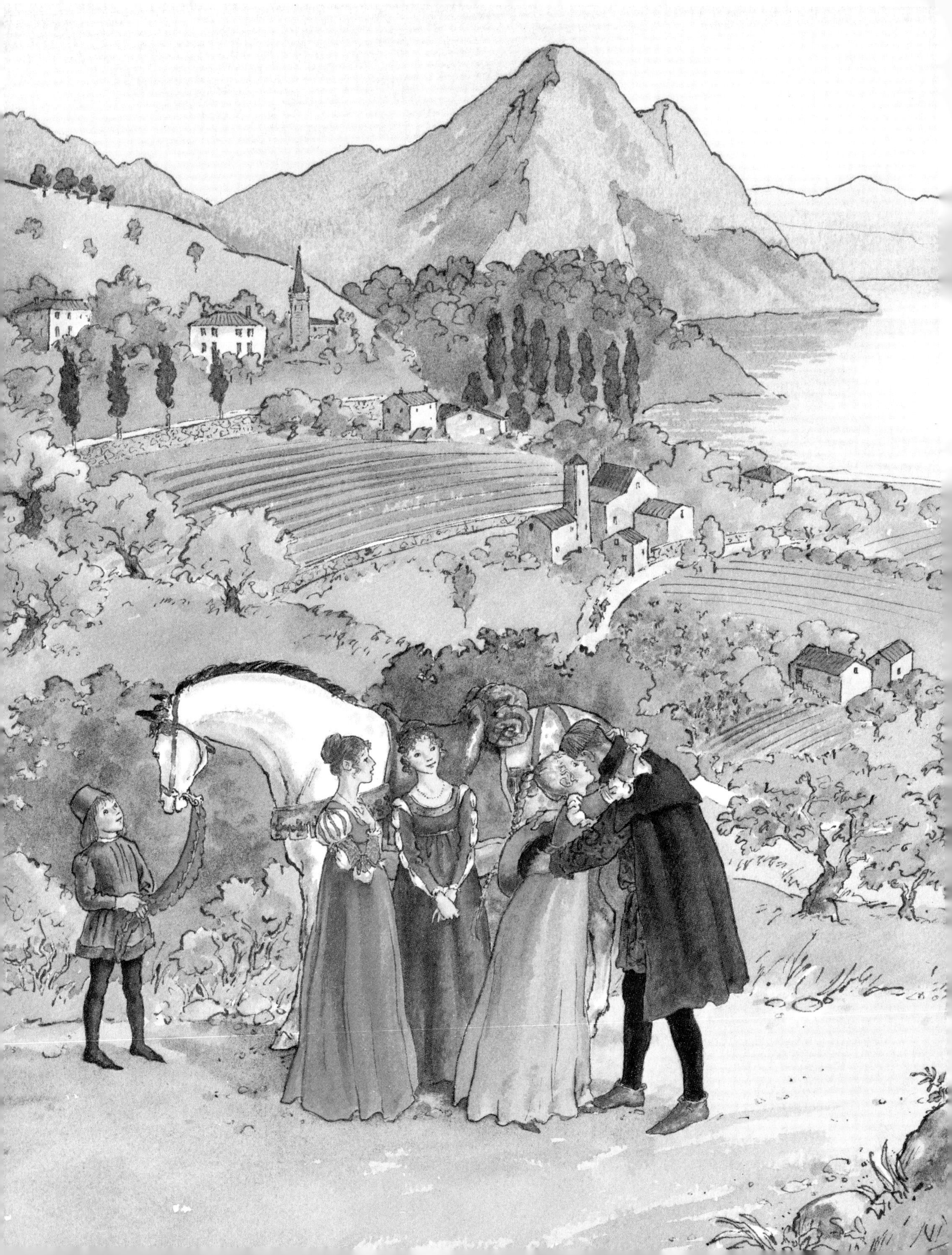

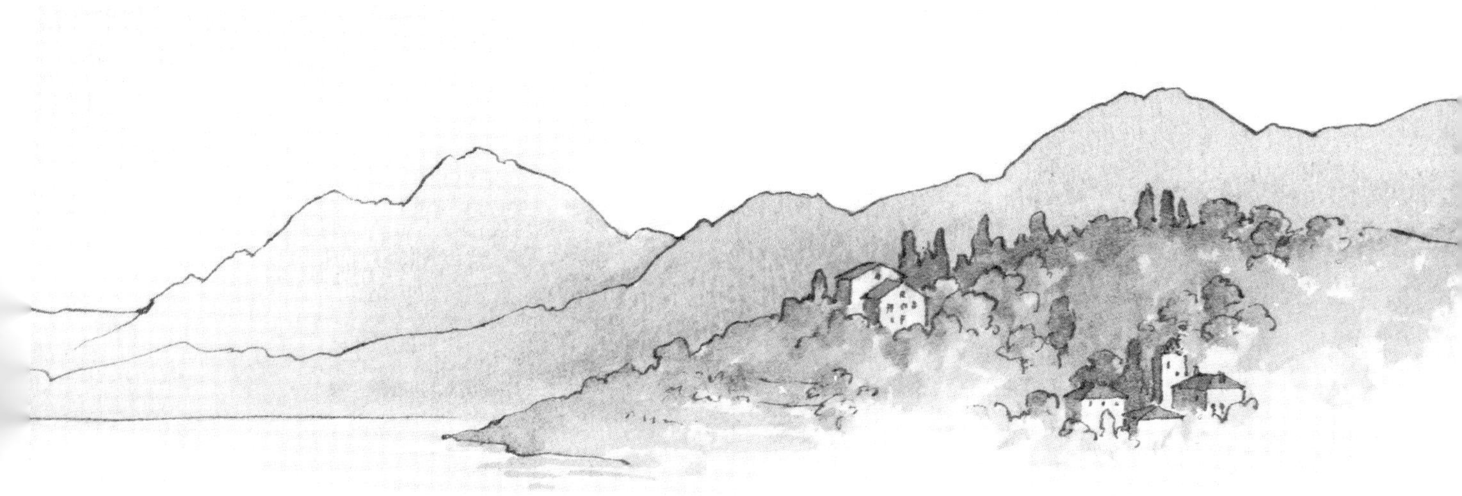

Long ago and far away, in a handsome house that overlooked the sea, there lived a rich merchant and his three daughters. Now, as often happens with merchants, it came time for him to leave town on business.

"Before going," he said to his daughters, "I shall give each of you a present, so you will be happy while I am away. What is it you want?"

The girls talked this over together and decided they wanted gold, silver, and silk to use for their spinning. Their father had gold, silver, and silk brought to them. He admonished them to behave while he was away and then departed.

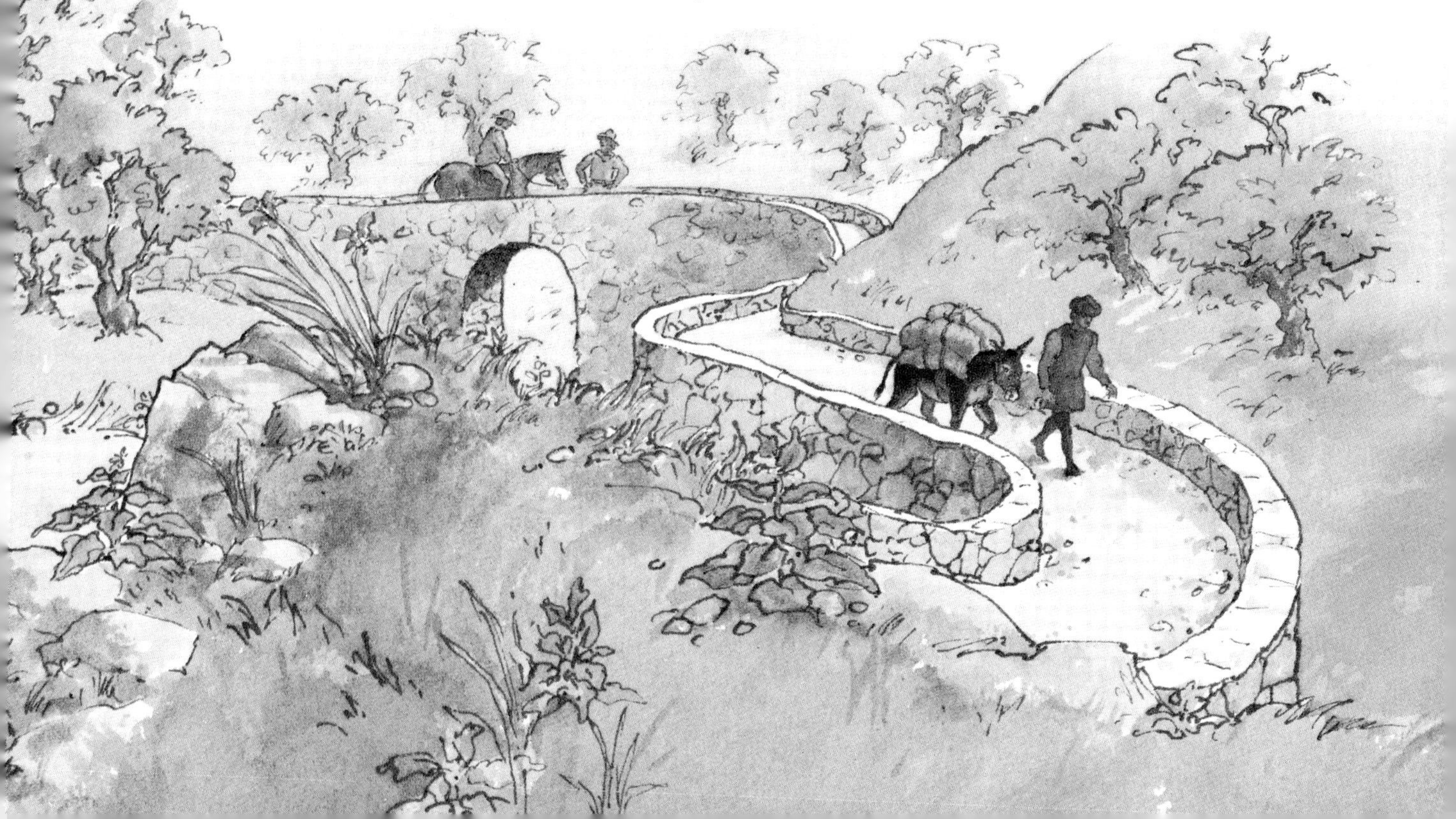

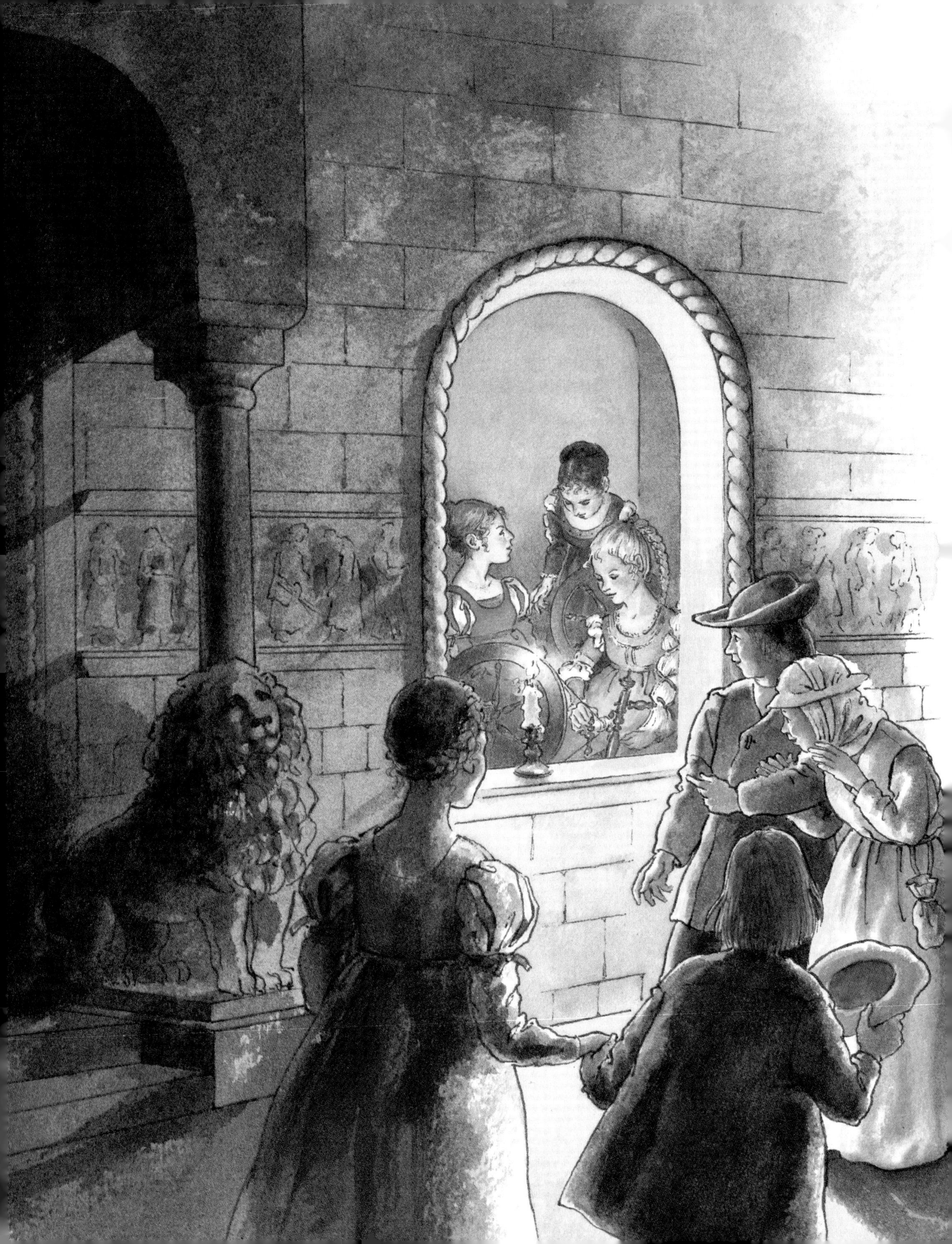

The name of the youngest sister was Giricoccola, and she was envied by her sisters because of her beauty. As was their habit, the elder sisters took what they wanted first. The oldest took the gold to spin, the middle sister took the silver, and that left only the silk for Giricoccola.

After supper, the three girls went to the window that overlooked the street and sat down at their wheels to spin. The villagers, out for a breath of air, stared at Giricoccola, as they did every evening, because of her beauty.

Later that night, the moon rose, looked in the window, and remarked:

Lovely the one who spins with gold,
lovelier still who silver spins;
but the spinner of silk surpasses all.

When they heard this, the two elder sisters were enraged, and determined that the next day they would exchange threads. So the following evening, they took the gold and silk, leaving only the silver for Giricoccola. As before, the moon rose, looked in the window, and remarked:

> *Lovely the one who spins with gold,*
> *lovelier still who silk does spin;*
> *but the spinner of silver surpasses all.*

Infuriated, the two older girls taunted Giricoccola. Such was her sweet nature that she endured their jeers without a word of complaint. This further angered the older sisters, who determined that the following evening they would once again switch threads to see what the moon would say.

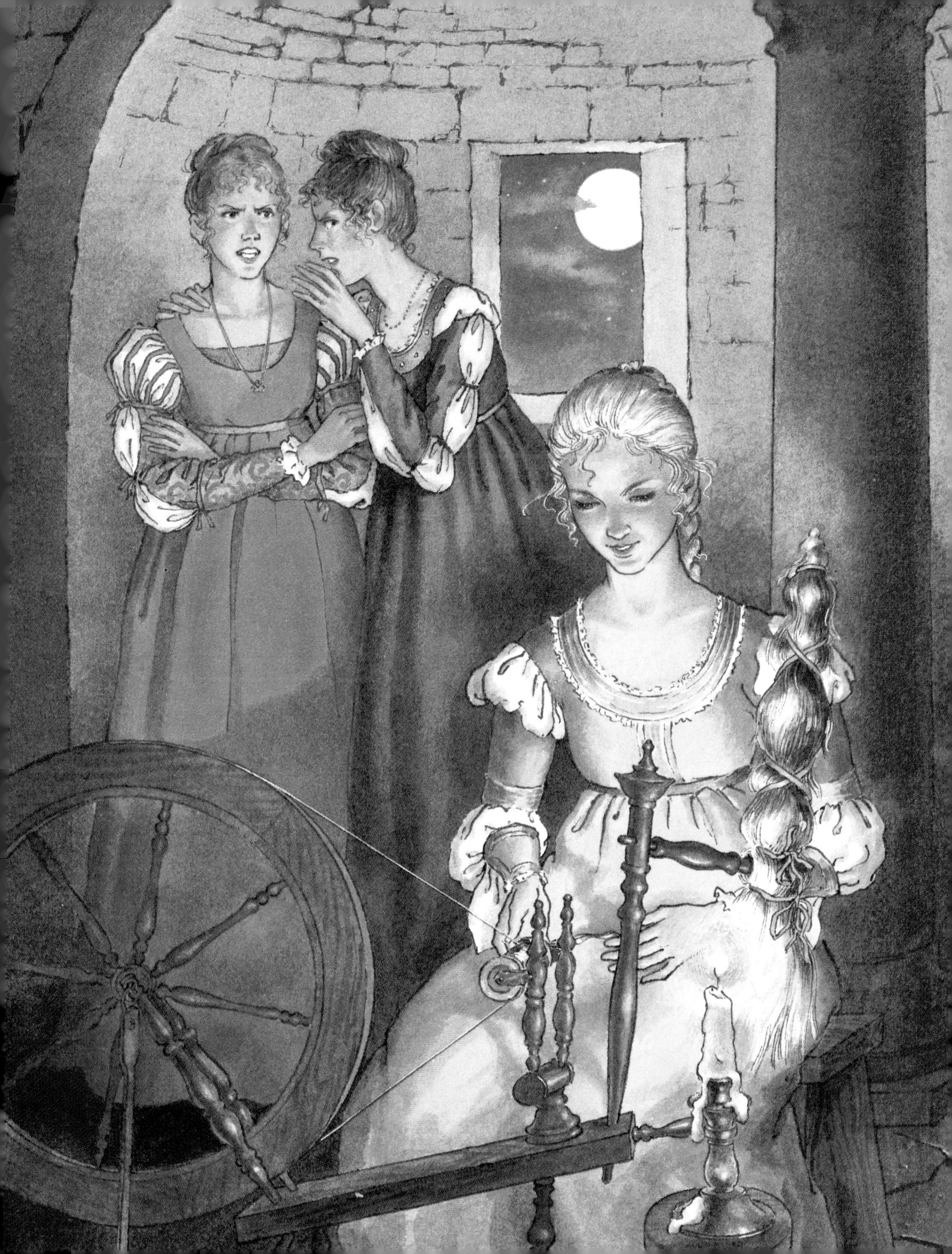

As soon as they finished supper, the girls once again took up their wheels in the window. This time Giricoccola was left the gold to spin. The minute the moon rose, she peered in the window and remarked:

> *Lovely the one who silver spins,*
> *lovelier still who spins with silk;*
> *but the spinner of gold surpasses all.*

This so angered the spiteful sisters that they took Giricoccola out and locked her in the hayloft.

The poor girl sat there weeping until she noticed that the moon had opened the shutter covering the window with a moonbeam.

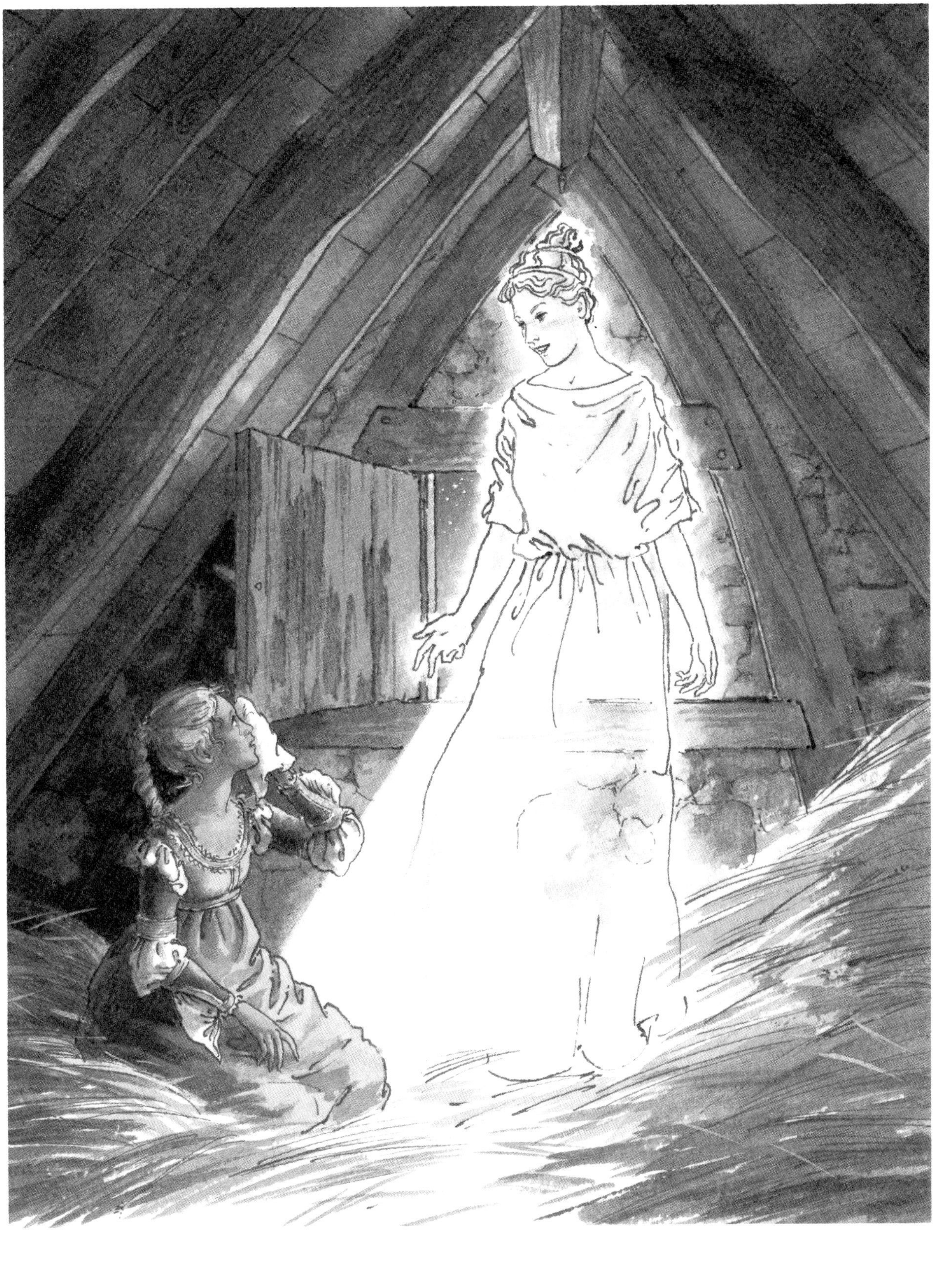

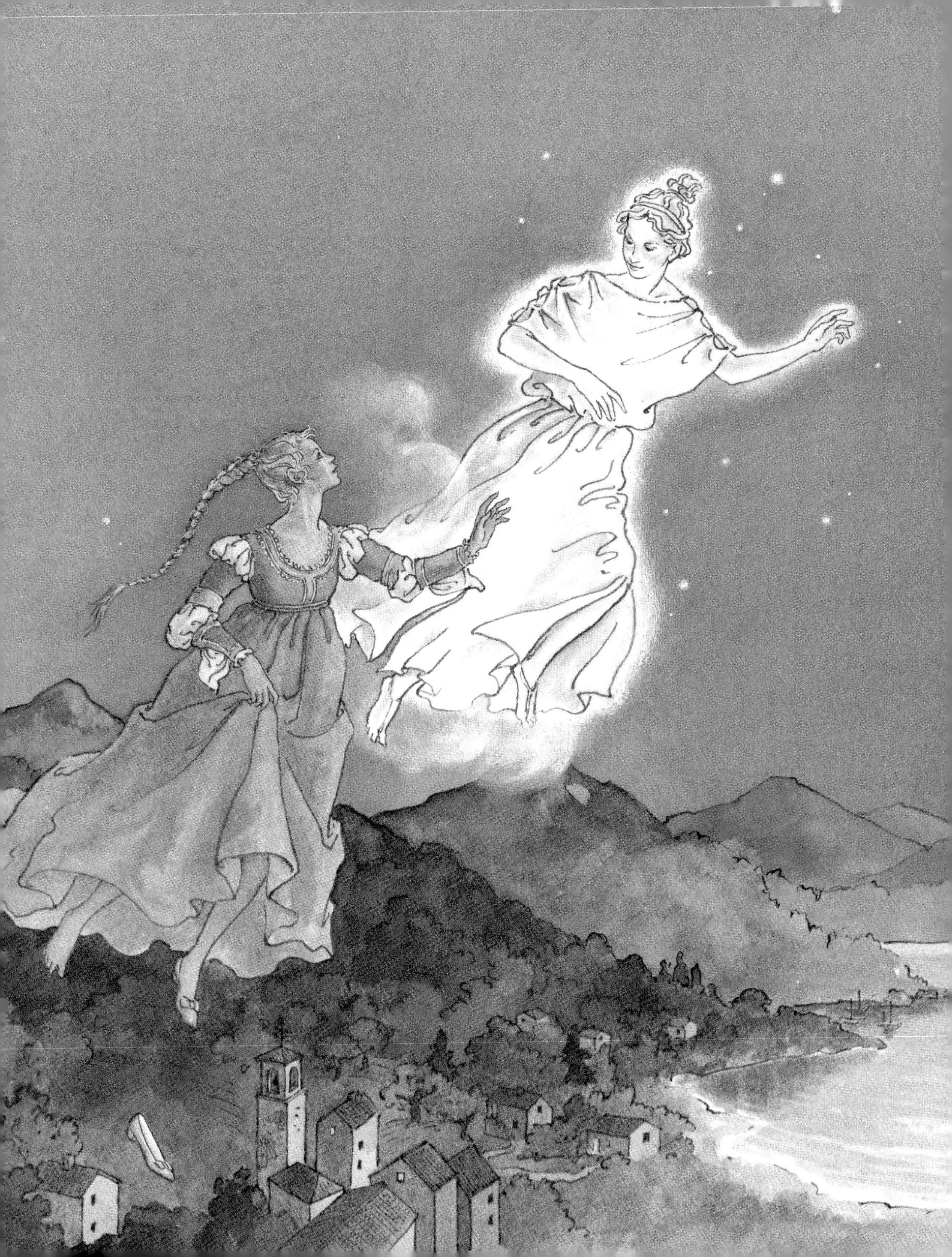

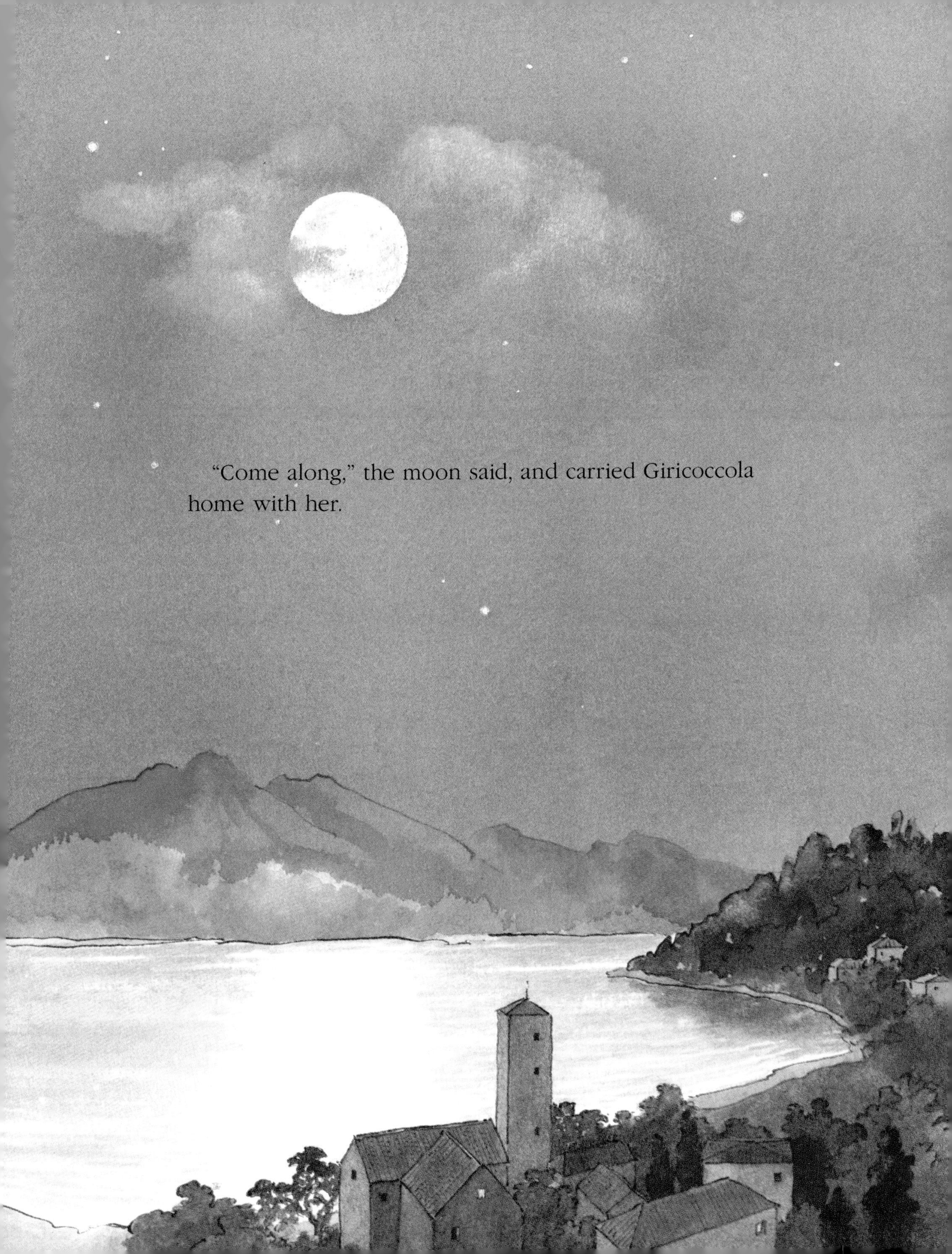

"Come along," the moon said, and carried Giricoccola home with her.

The next evening, the two sisters sat spinning by themselves in the window. The moon rose, looked in the window, and remarked:

> *Lovely the one who spins with gold,*
> *lovelier still who silver spins;*
> *but the one at my house surpasses all.*

At that the sisters went raging off to the hayloft to see what was what. Giricoccola was gone! They went to see the town witch so she could explain what had happened. After consulting her magic book, she told them that Giricoccola was at the moon's house, living more comfortably than they were.

"How can we change her good fortune to bad?" asked the sisters.

"Leave it all to me," said the witch, who conjured up a tray of magic brooches, disguised herself as a gypsy, and went to peddle her wares beneath the moon's window.

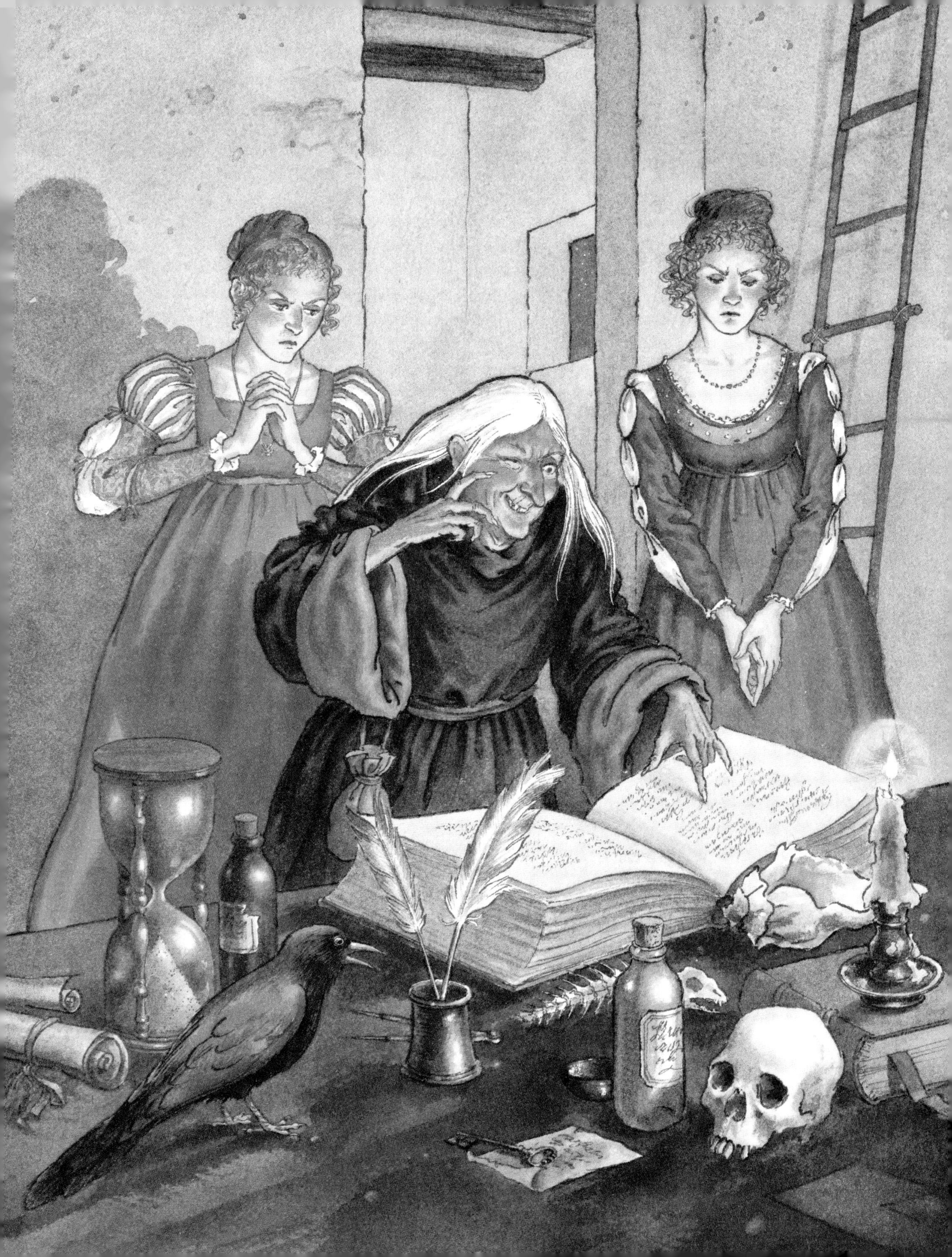

Giricoccola looked out the window. The witch said, "Would you like a beautiful brooch? I'll let you have one for a penny."

Now the brooches were truly beautiful, and Giricoccola invited the witch inside. "Here, let me fasten one to your gown," the evil woman said.

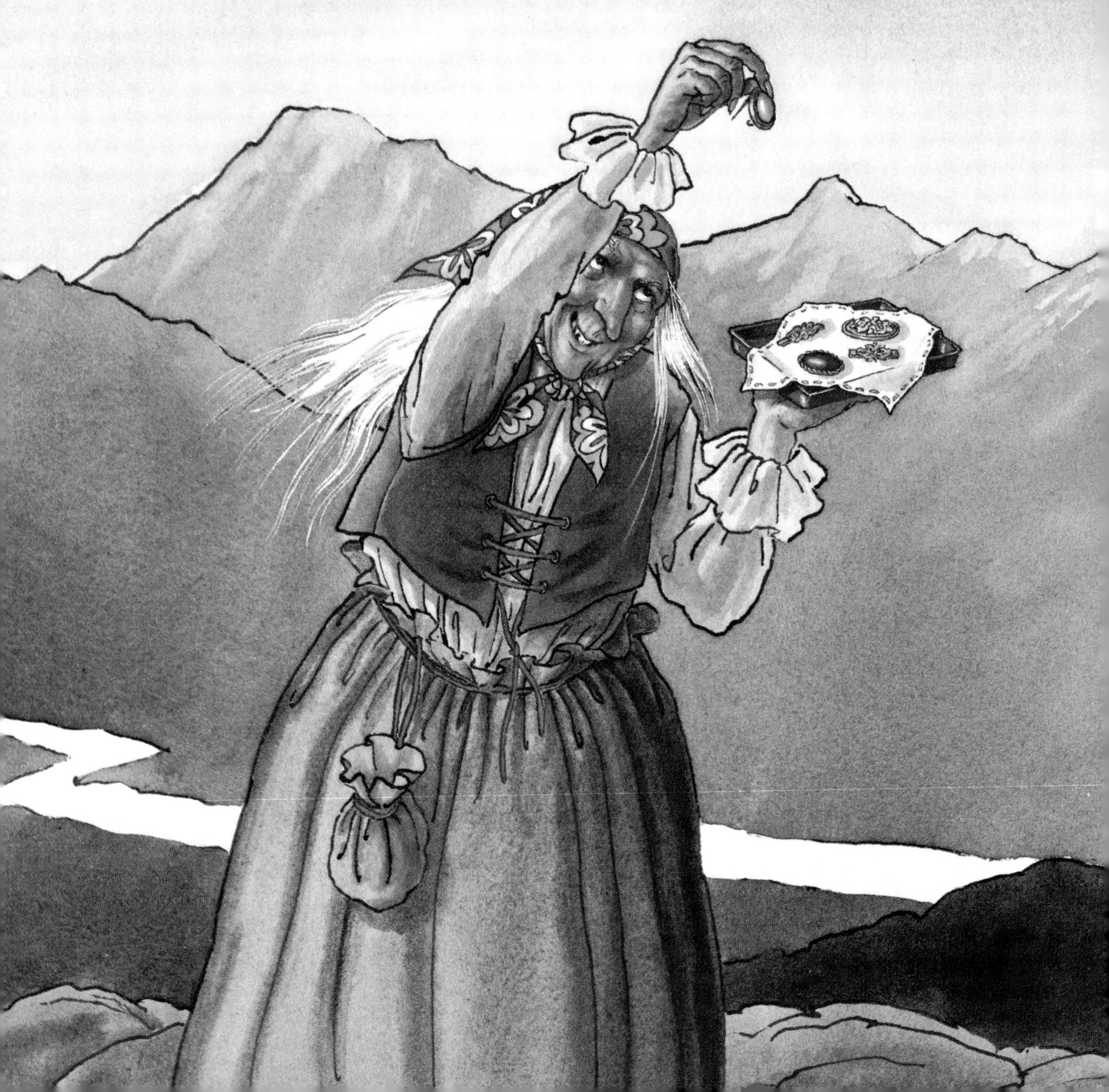

The moment she thrust the pin into Giricoccola's dress, the girl turned into a statue and the old woman ran off to report to the sisters.

When the moon returned from her trip around the world, she found Giricoccola turned into a statue. "Didn't I tell you to let no one in," she scolded. "I should leave you like this for disobeying me."

Despite her stern words, the moon was softhearted, and she finally relented. When she drew the pin from Giricoccola's gown, the girl came back to life and promised never to let anyone into the house again.

Some time later, the two sisters returned to the witch to ask about Giricoccola. The witch consulted her magic book and said that, for some strange reason, the girl was alive and well. So the sisters implored the evil woman to change her into a statue once more.

This time the witch conjured up a tray of magic combs to peddle beneath Giricoccola's window. They were too attractive to resist, and Giricoccola called the old woman inside.

The moment the witch woman ran a comb through Giricoccola's hair, the girl turned back into a statue. Laughing delightedly, the witch ran home to tell the sisters.

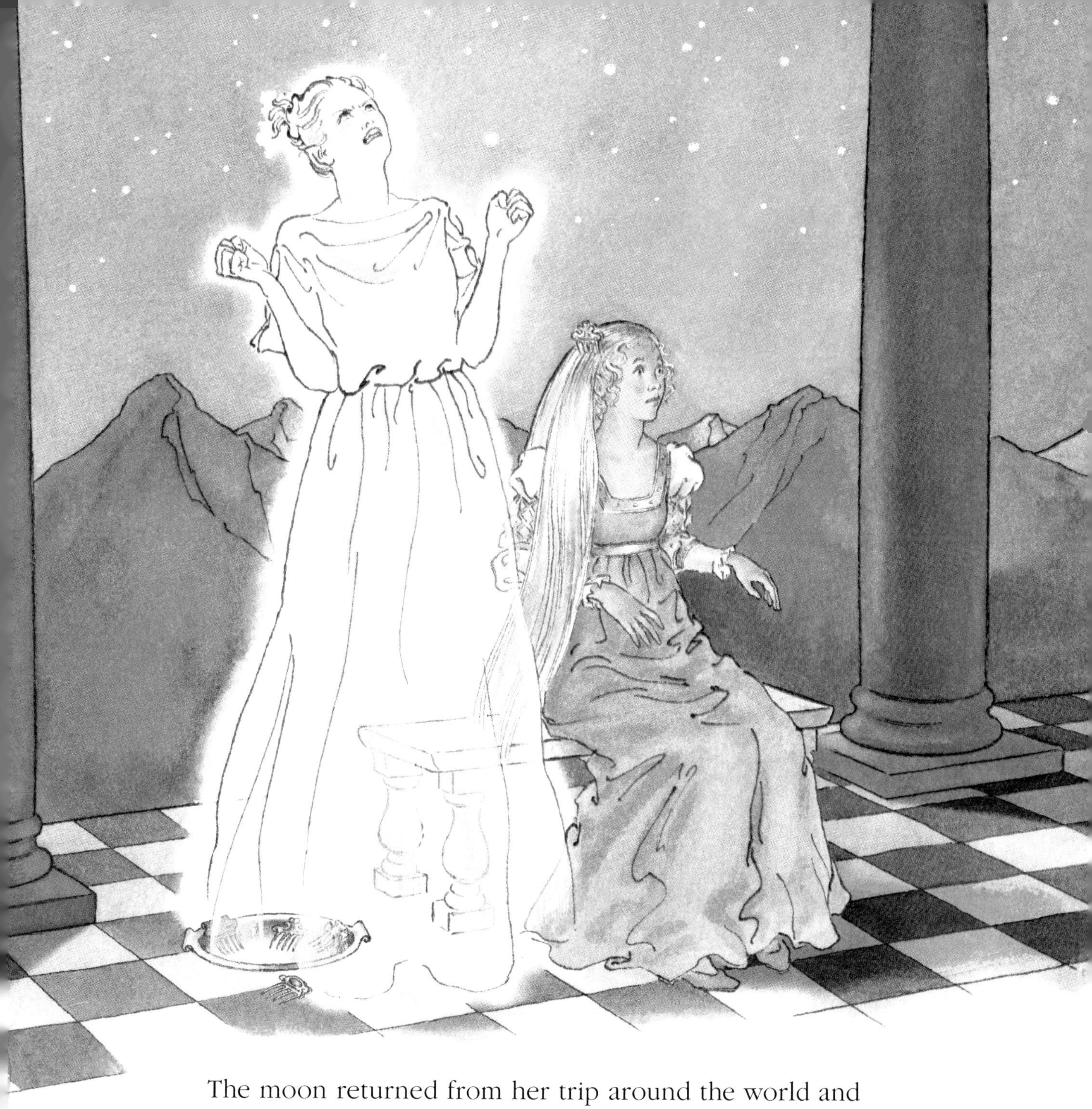

The moon returned from her trip around the world and was angry to discover that the poor girl had become a statue once more. When she had calmed down, the moon forgave Giricoccola again and removed the comb, and the girl revived. "But if this happens again," the moon warned, "I'll let you remain a statue."

Giricoccola solemnly promised not to let in anyone.

Some time later, the sisters again consulted with the witch, who learned from her book that Giricoccola was alive and well.

So she conjured up a beautiful embroidered gown and went off to the moon's house yet a third time. Giricoccola could not resist the charming gown, and the moment she slipped it over her head, she turned into a statue.

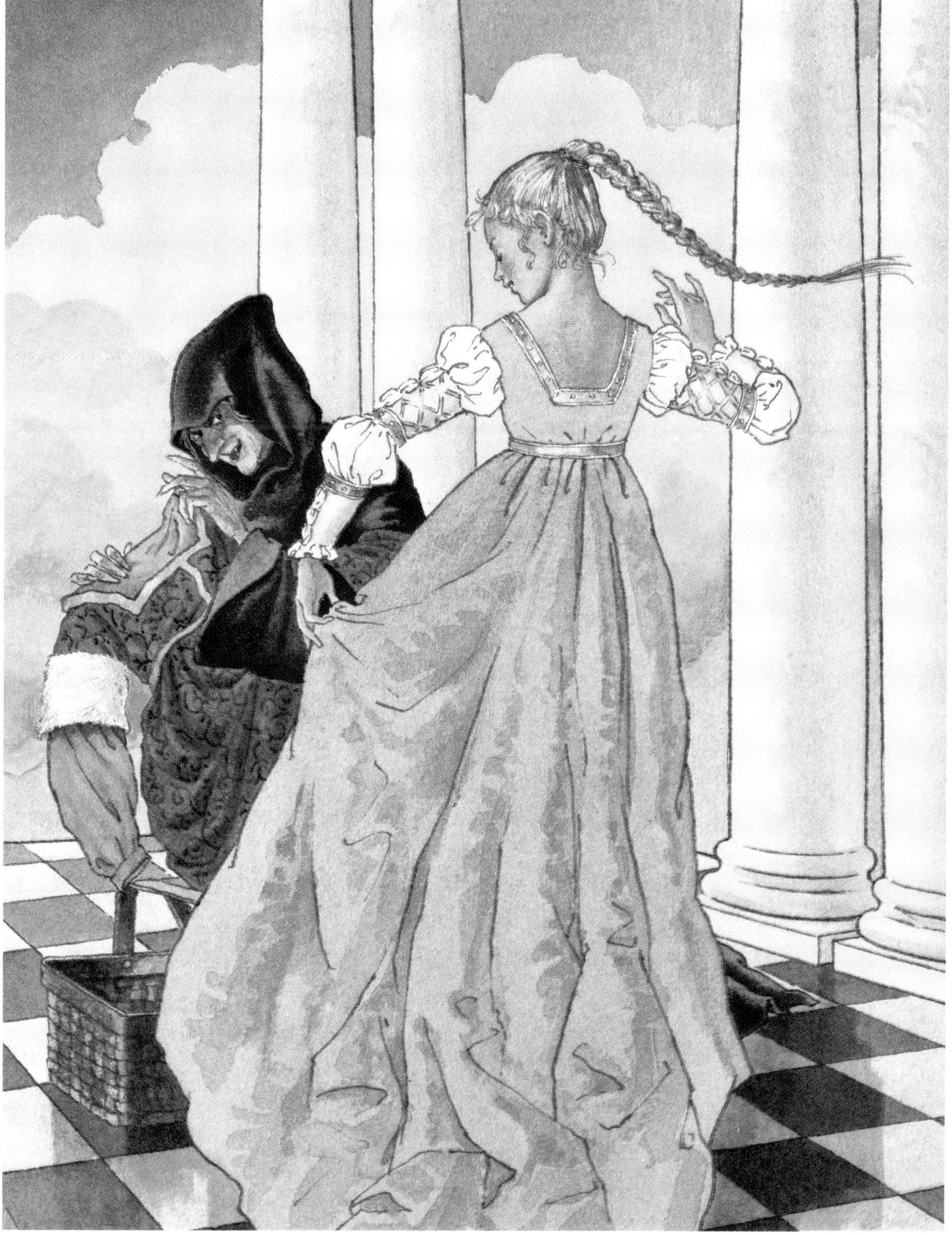

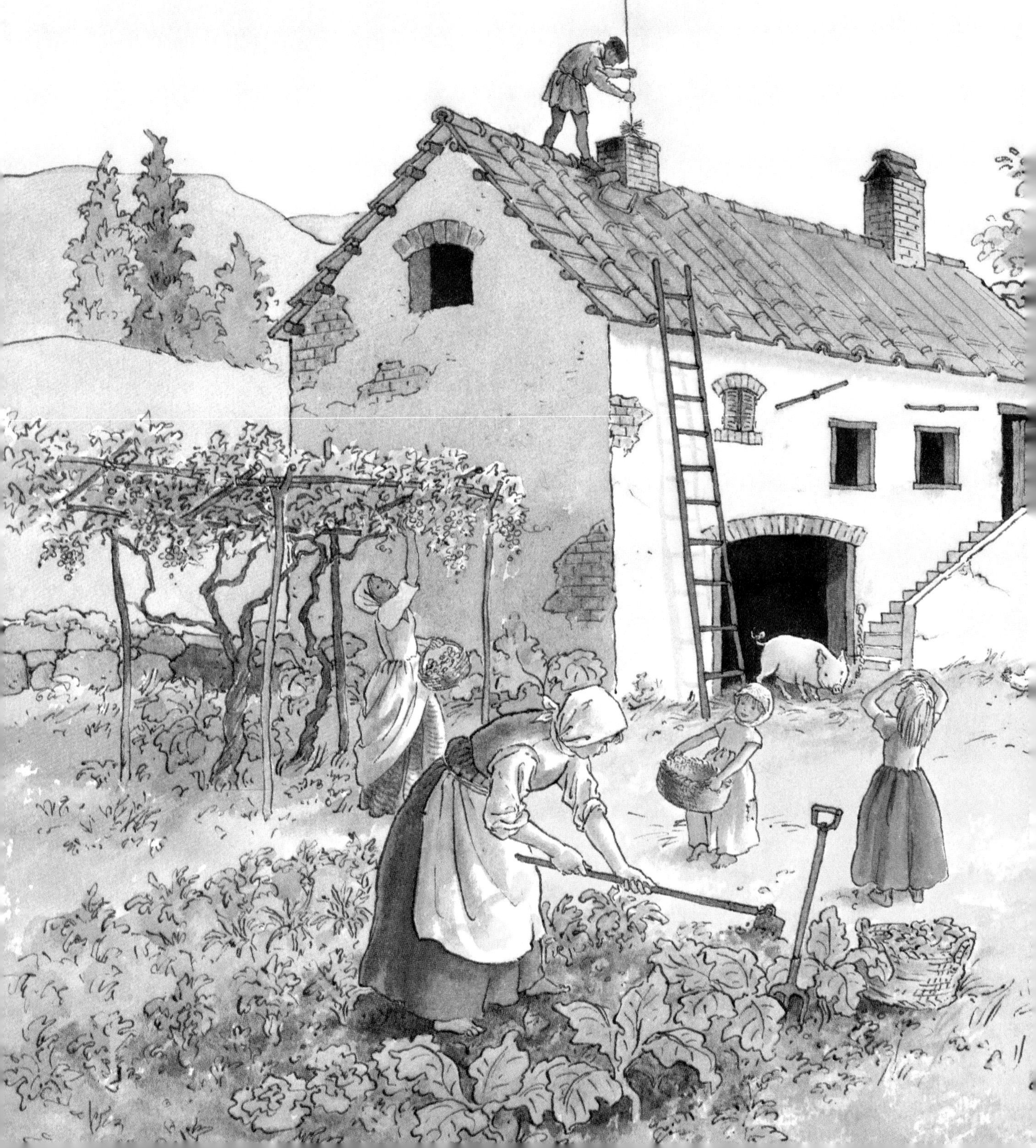

This time, when the moon returned home, she washed her hands of the matter and sold the statue for a few pennies to a chimney sweep. Now the sweep was so delighted with his purchase that he took the statue along as he went about his work, tying it to his donkey's saddle.

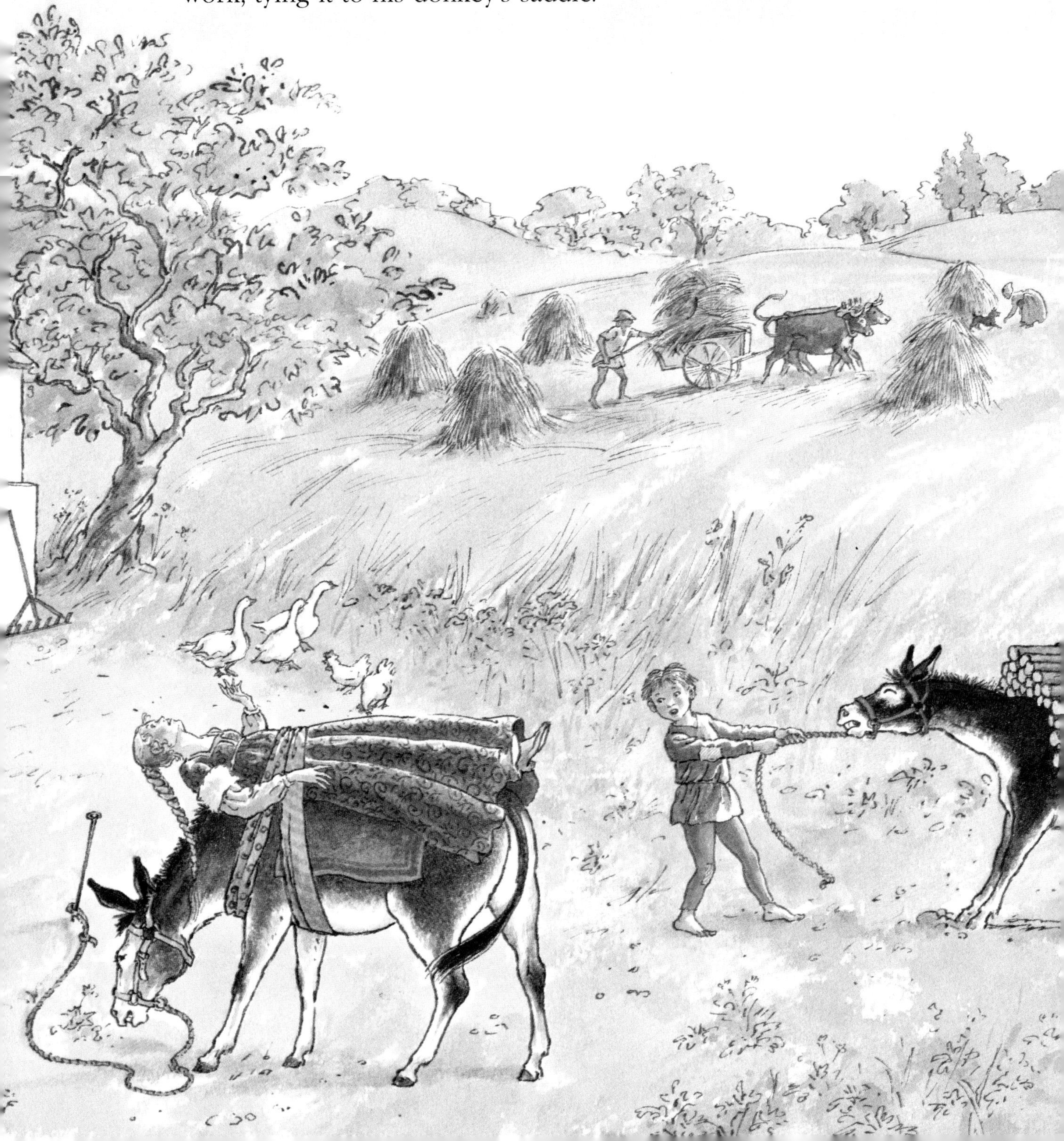

One day a king's son happened by. He saw the beautiful statue and fell in love with it at a glance. He was so determined to have the statue that he paid the chimney sweep the statue's weight in gold and took it home, where he kept it in his room. Whenever he left the room, he locked the door to protect his beloved statue.

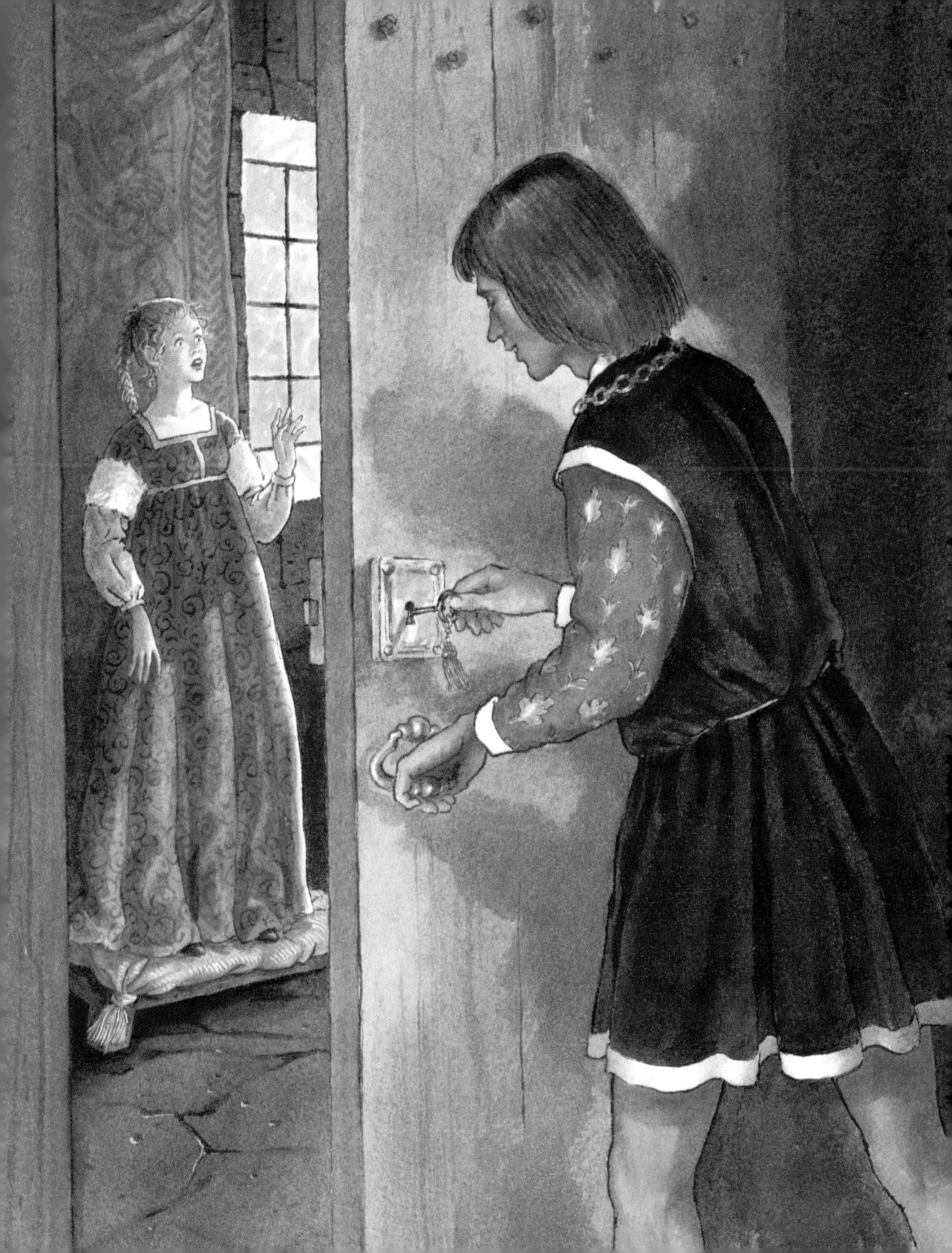

One day, Giricoccola's sisters were invited to a ball. Remembering the beautiful gown the witch had made, they went to her to find out where it was so they might copy it. Her magic book told them, so they went to the prince's room while he was away, used a skeleton key to get in, and lifted the dress off the statue. Before anyone could discover them, they hurried away.

In a moment, Giricoccola stirred and came back to life. When the king's son returned, he was frantic to discover that his statue was missing. But Giricoccola jumped out from behind the door where she was hiding and explained everything from beginning to end.

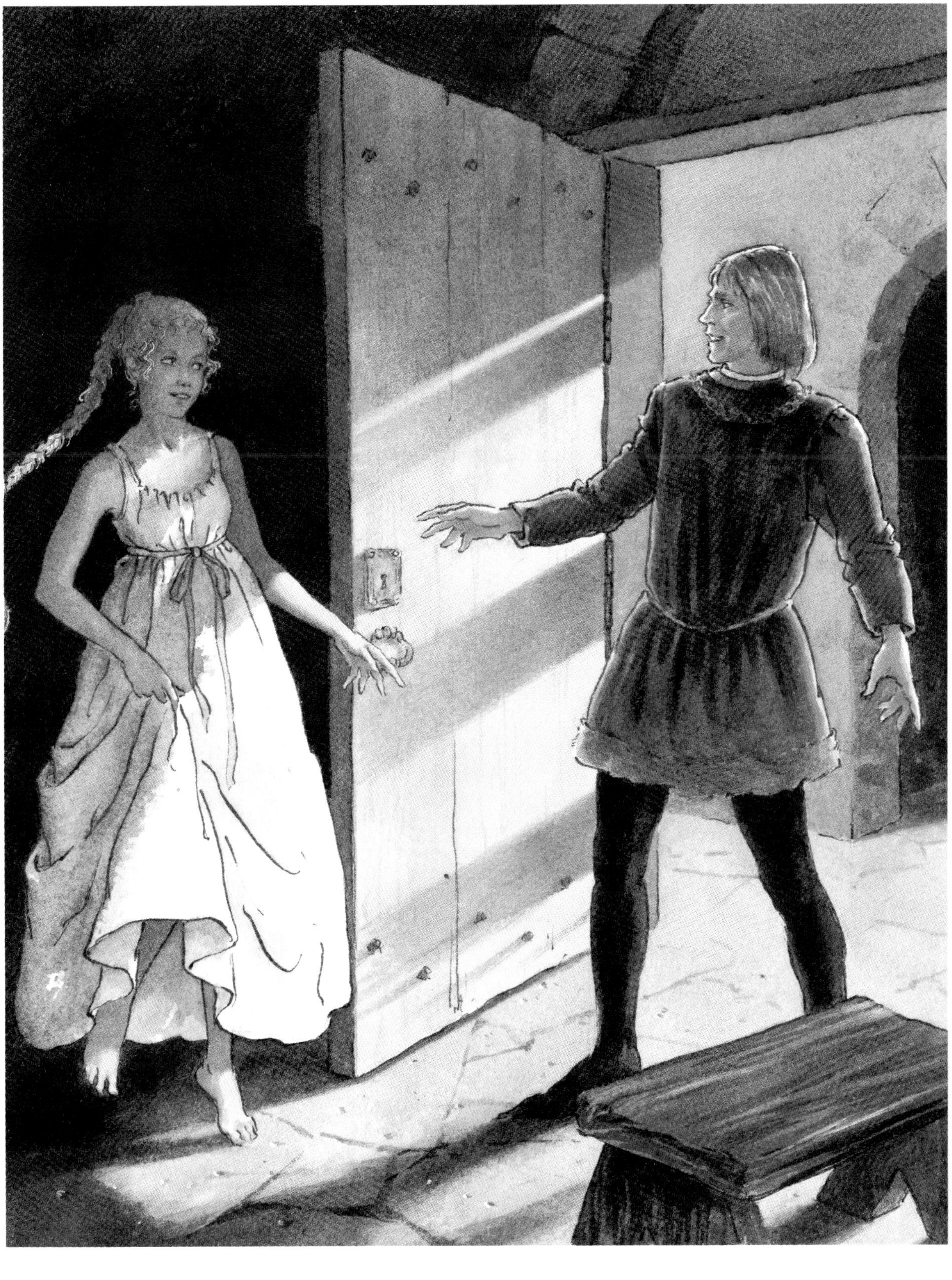

The prince took Giricoccola to his parents, who loved her at first sight, and the wedding was celebrated at once.

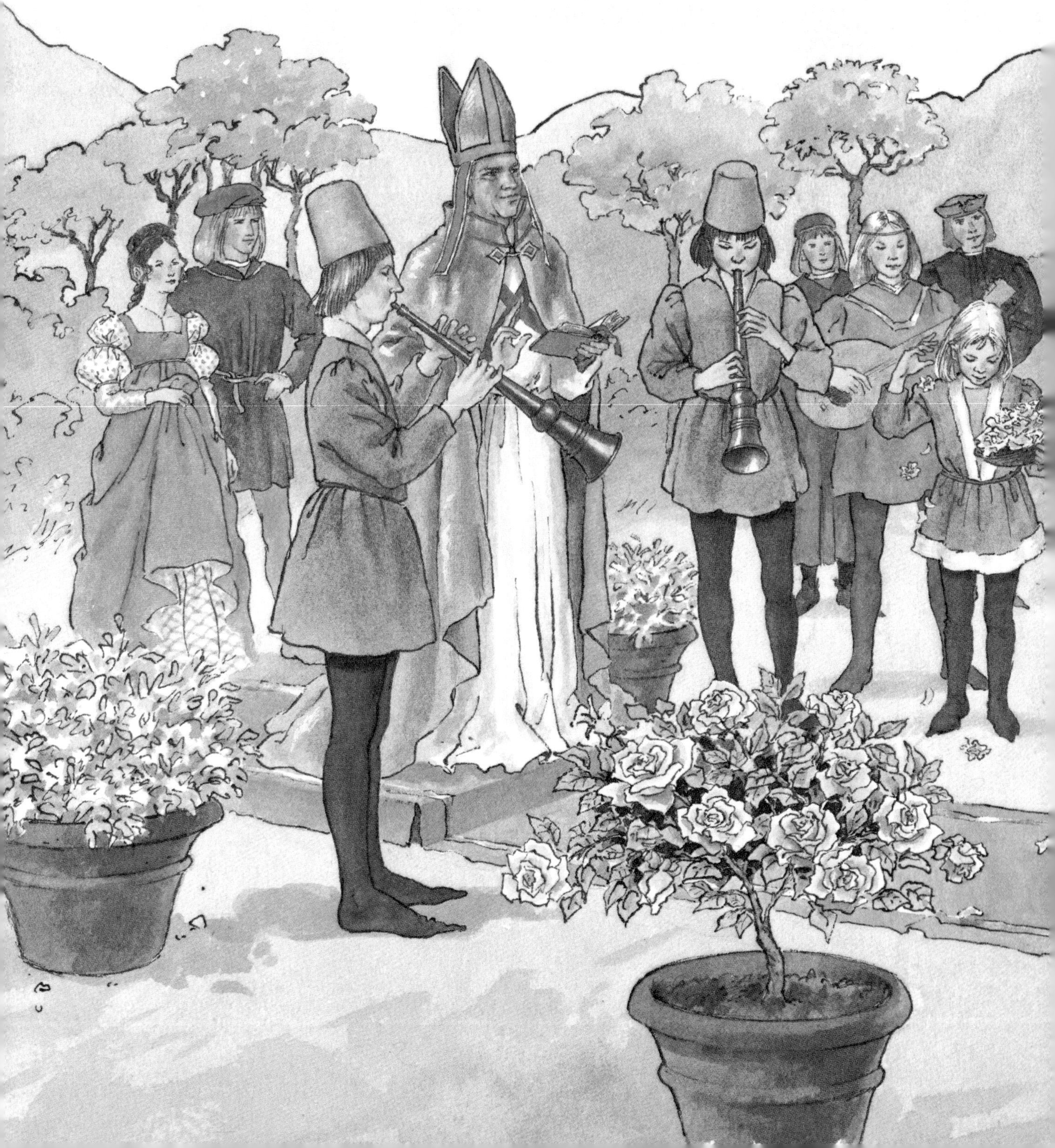

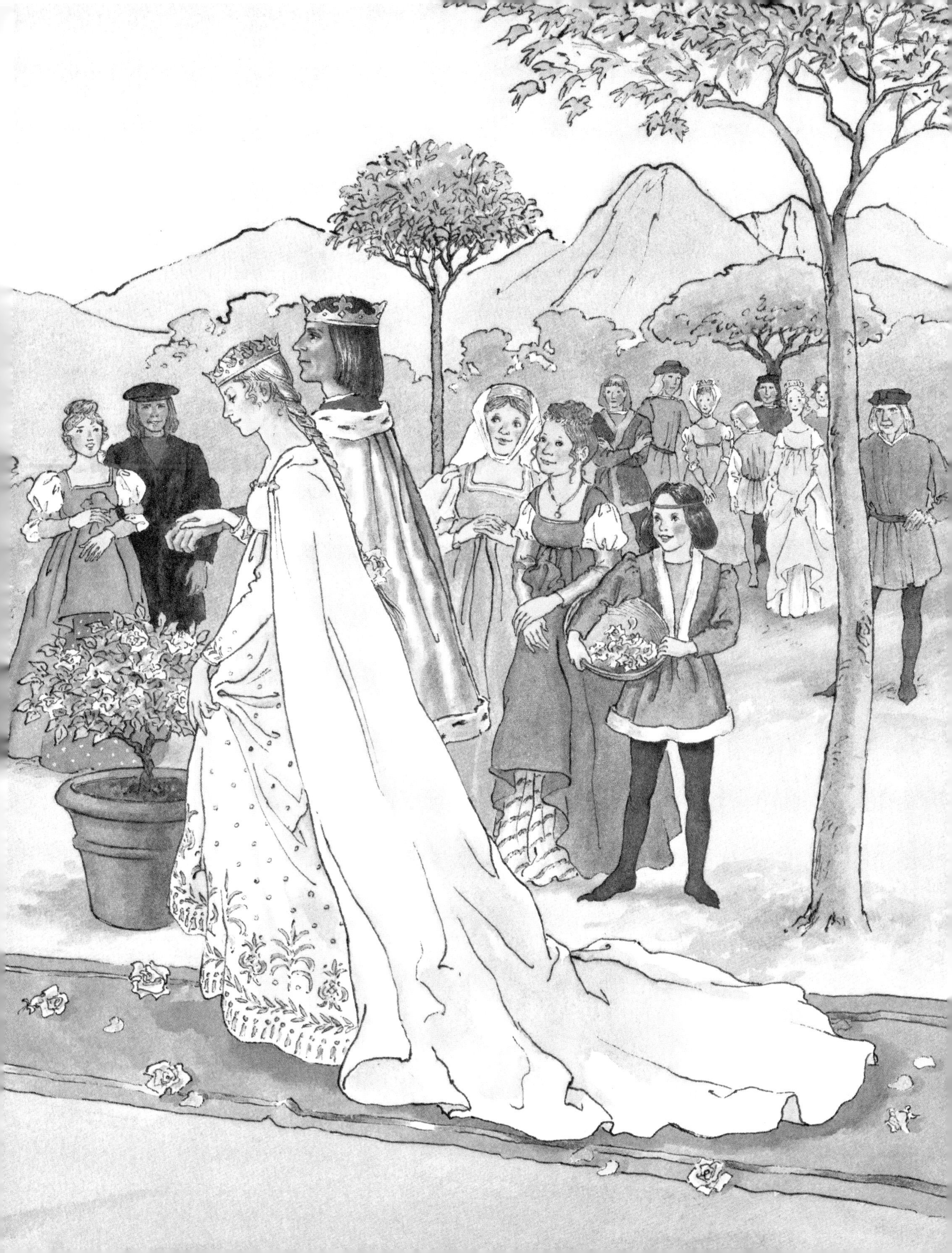

It was not until some time later that Giricoccola's sisters went again to the witch. Her book told them all that had happened, and they died of rage right then and there.

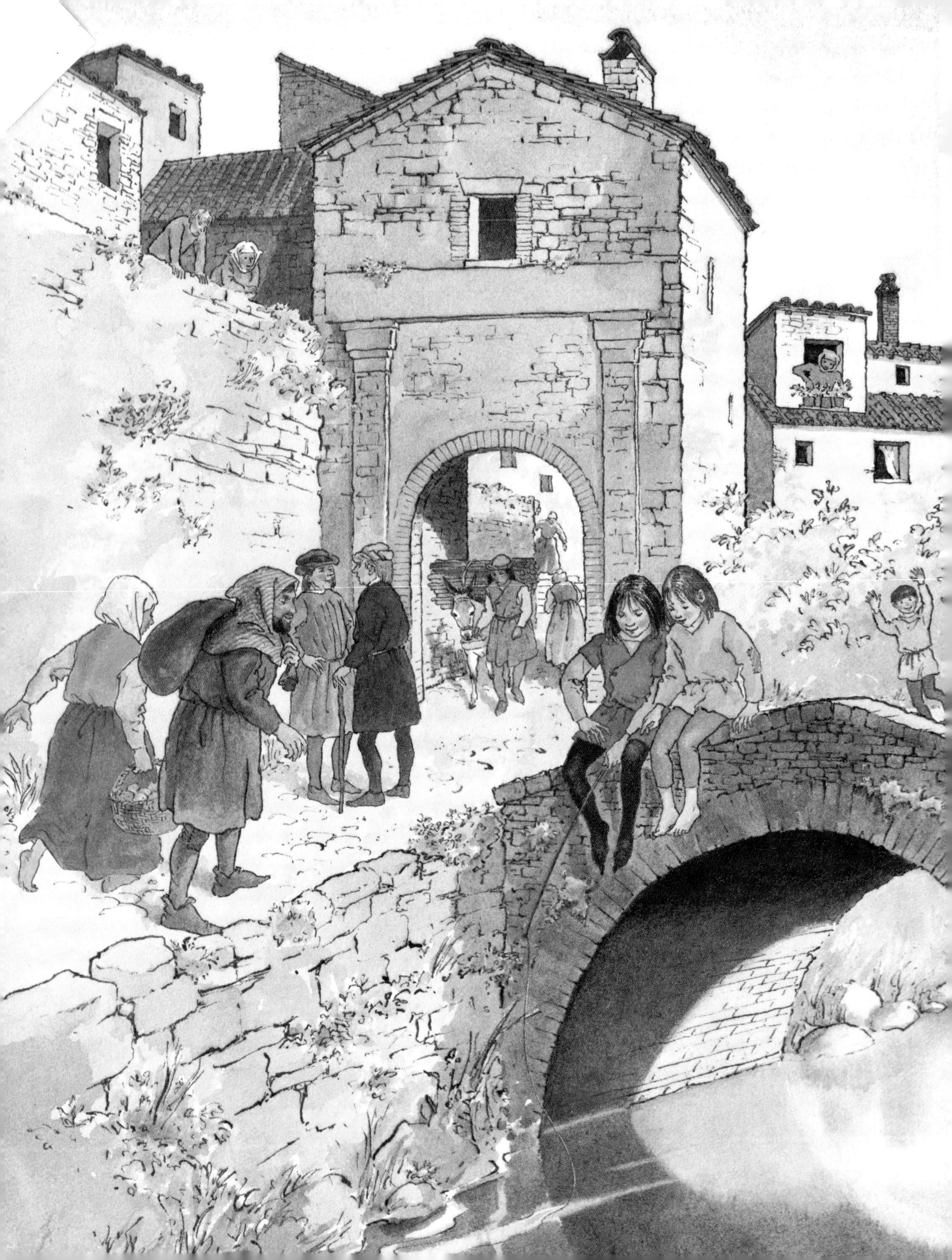